For Aunt Patti,
whose spirit of friendship and humor
inspires me every day—AB

PENGUIN WORKSHOP
An Imprint of Penguin Random House LLC, New York

Copyright © 2021 by Ashley Belote. All rights reserved. Published by Penguin Workshop, an imprint of Penguin Random House LLC, New York. PENGUIN and PENGUIN WORKSHOP are trademarks of Penguin Books Ltd, and the W colophon is a registered trademark of Penguin Random House LLC. Manufactured in China.

Visit us online at www.penguinrandomhouse.com.

Library of Congress Control Number: 2021007170

ISBN 9780593384824 (paperback)        10 9 8 7 6 5 4 3 2 1
ISBN 9780593384855 (library binding)    10 9 8 7 6 5 4 3 2 1

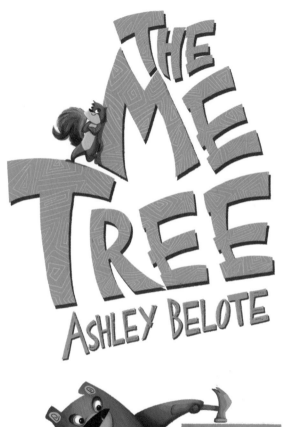

# THE ME TREE

## ASHLEY BELOTE

Penguin Workshop

This is simply unbearable!
No space. No privacy.

It may be time to leave the cave life behind
and find some space. A space *just for me*.

**COMMUNITY CAVE SPACES AVAILABLE!**

Flexible payment options
*Great for hibernation*
Located over the river
and through the woods,
obviously. ↓
HUNDREDS OF ROOMMATES! →AVOID ALONE TIME!←

GET YOUR SPACE BEFORE THEY'RE GONE!

COZY CAVE WALL VIEWS
Move in TODAY!!!

1-800-ILOVECAVES

**SEEKING ROOFMATE!**
Yes, <u>roof</u>mate.
I'm a bird, so
I live on the roof.

**SEEKING SOLITUDE?
BUY A
TREE HOUSE
TODAY!**

-MOVE-IN READY!-

*utilities ON!*
*Fully furnished!*

FOR SALE

CREDIT CHECK REQUIRED!!!

**FOR RENT!
BIRDHOUSE**
*No squirrels, please*
utilities & cable included! Call:
1-800-BIRDSRULE

Hmm . . . no roommates?
An entire tree that's all mine?

A tree just for me!
I think I'll call it . . .
The Me Tree!

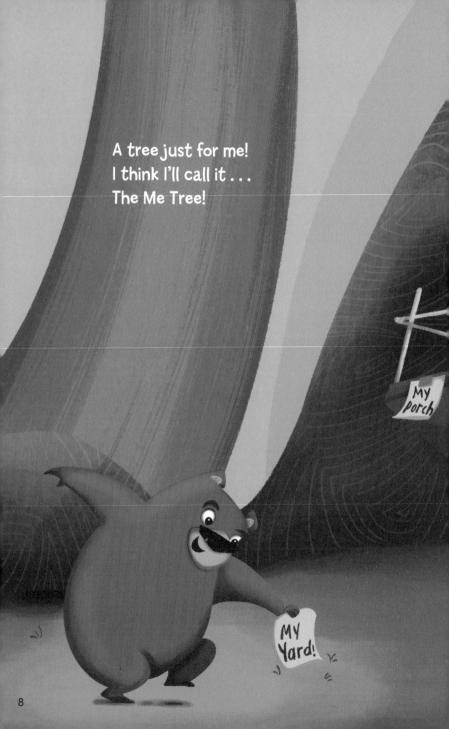

My Porch

My Yard!

8

Wait . . . what? Who's in my tree?
It's not just me!

Squirrels?!
No wonder there wasn't any popcorn left . . .
I need a minute to myself.

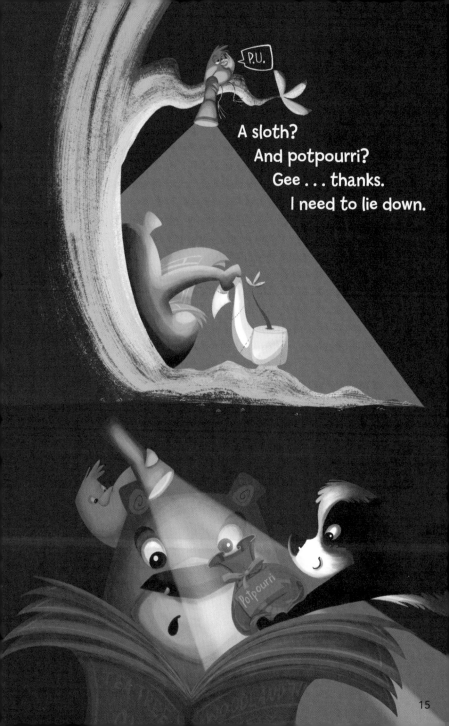

Bees! You already make it
hard for me to get honey . . .
now you're disturbing my dreams!
I need a good soak.

16

And now there's a manatee.
You've got to be kidding me—
that's my loofah! It's definitely
not just me in my tree!

IT'S NEVER,

EVER, EVER, **EVER**

JUST ME
IN MY TREE!

I just want to be . . .

ALONE!

Dear B,
I cleaned
the
chimney...

THE ME
TREE

Can't you see?
**THE ME TREE!**

Finally.
It's just me in my tree.
No squirrels.

No sloth.

No manatee.

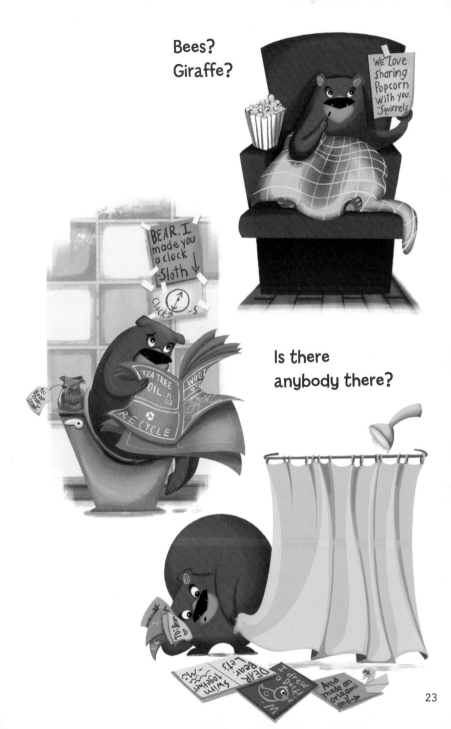

Nope. Just me . . . in my tree.
This isn't as fun as I thought it would be.

# I think it's time for a change . . .

and I have *just* the idea.

Let's turn
The *Me* Tree into . . .

The **We** Tree!